APR 2 2 2011

P9-EDM-257

NAPA CITY-COUNTY LIBRARY
580 COOMBS STREET
NAPA, CA 94559

ROSEMARY WELLS

TIMOTHY GOES TO SCHOOL

PUFFIN BOOKS

PUFFIN BOOKS
Published by the Penguin Group
Penguin Putnam Books for Young Readers, 345 Hudson Street, New York, New York 10014, U.S.A.
Penguin Books Ltd, 27 Wrights Lane, London W8 5TZ, England
Penguin Books Australia Ltd, Ringwood, Victoria, Australia
Penguin Books Canada Ltd, 10 Alcorn Avenue, Toronto, Ontario, Canada M4V 3B2
Penguin Books (N.Z.) Ltd, 182-190 Wairau Road, Auckland 10, New Zealand

Penguin Books Ltd, Registered Offices: Harmondsworth, Middlesex, England

First published in the United States of America by Dial Books for Young Readers,
a division of Penguin Books USA Inc., 1981

This edition with new illustrations published by Viking,
a division of Penguin Putnam Books for Young Readers, 2000

Published by Puffin Books, a division of Penguin Putnam Books for Young Readers, 2000

11

Copyright © Rosemary Wells, 1981, 2000
All rights reserved

THE LIBRARY OF CONGRESS HAS CATALOGED THE DIAL EDITION AS FOLLOWS:
Wells, Rosemary / Timothy goes to school.
Summary: Timothy learns about being accepted and making friends
during the first week of his first year at school.
[1. School stories.] I. Title.
PZ7.W46843Ti [E] 80-20785
ISBN 0-8037-8948-3 / ISBN 0-8037-8949-1 (lib. bdg.)

Puffin Books ISBN 0-14-056742-9

Manufactured in China

Except in the United States of America, this book is sold subject
to the condition that it shall not, by way of trade or otherwise,
be lent, re-sold, hired out, or otherwise circulated without the
publisher's prior consent in any form of binding or cover other than
that in which it is published and without a similar condition including
this condition being imposed on the subsequent purchaser.

The art for this book was prepared in the usual way: with watercolor,
pen and ink, gouache, pastel, and rubber stamps.

For Mimi Kayden

TIMOTHY'S mother made him a brand-new sunsuit for the first day of school.

"Hooray!" said Timothy.

Timothy went to school in his new sunsuit
with his new book and his new pencil.

"Good morning!" said Timothy.
"Good morning!" said Mrs. Jenkins.

"Timothy," said Mrs. Jenkins, "this is Claude. Claude, this is Timothy. I'm sure you'll be the best of friends."

A B C D E F G H

"Hello!" said Timothy.
"Nobody wears a sunsuit on the first day of
school," said Claude.

During playtime Timothy hoped and
hoped that Claude would fall into a puddle.

But he didn't.

When Timothy came home, his mother asked,
"How was school today?"

"Nobody wears a sunsuit on the first day of school," said Timothy.

"I will make you a beautiful new jacket," said Timothy's mother.

Timothy wore his new jacket the next day.

"Hello!" said Timothy to Claude.
"You're not supposed to wear party clothes
on the second day of school," said Claude.

All day Timothy wanted and wanted Claude
to make a mistake.

But he didn't.

When Timothy went home, his mother asked,
"How did it go?"

"You're not supposed to wear party clothes
on the second day of school," said Timothy.
"Don't worry," said Timothy's mother.
"Tomorrow you just wear something in-between
like everyone else."

The next day Timothy went to school in his favorite shirt.

"Look!" said Timothy. "You are wearing the same shirt I am!"

"No," said Claude, "*you* are wearing the same shirt that *I* am."

During lunch Timothy wished and wished
that Claude would have to eat all alone.

But he didn't.

After school Timothy's mother could not find
Timothy. "Where are you?" she called.
"I'm never going back to school," said Timothy.
"Why not?" called his mother.

"Because Claude is the smartest and the best at everything and he has all the friends," said Timothy.

"You'll feel better in your new football shirt," said Timothy's mother.

Timothy did not feel better in his new
football shirt.

That morning Claude played the saxophone.
"I can't stand it anymore," said a voice next to
Timothy.

It was Violet.

"You can't stand what?" Timothy asked Violet.

"Grace!" said Violet. "She sings. She dances. She counts up to a thousand and she sits next to me!"

During playtime Timothy and Violet
stayed together.

Violet said, "I can't believe you've been here all along!"

"Will you come home and have cookies with me after school?" Timothy asked.

On the way home Timothy and Violet laughed
so much about Claude and Grace that they both
got the hiccups.